THE TREAS... SOCK

by
Pat Thomson
Illustrated by
Tony Ross

VICTOR GOLLANCZ LTD
LONDON   1986

Mum,
on my way home,
I took off my sock.
Look.

Is that your sock?
It looks rather long
and it's shaped like a sausage.
Whatever is in this sock?

On my way home,
I found a frog.
The frog was brown and green and fat
so I put it in my sock.

Oh help!
A frog in a sock.
Put it in the garden.
What else is in this soggy sock?

Before I found the frog,
I found a little pig.
The pig was small and pink and lost
so I put it in my sock.

A pink, plastic pig, thank goodness.
At least it's not alive.
What else is in this shapeless sock?

Before I found the pig,
I found a big, brass button.
The button was round and bright
and shining
so I put it in my sock.

That's an unusual button.
Perhaps it came off a soldier's coat.
What else is in this special sock?

Before I found the button,
I found a good, glass marble.
Green and blue are caught inside
so I put it in my sock.

Lucky you!
A lovely, swirling marble.
What else is in this super sock?

Before I found the marble,
I found a heavy key.
The key was old and a funny shape
so I put it in my sock.

Well, now.
Perhaps it's the key
to a secret garden.
What else is in this sack of a sock?

Before I found the key,
I found a rubber band.
I had to save it to ping my friends
so I put it in my sock.

Really!
Mind your friends
don't ping you back.
What else is in this stretchy sock?

Before I found the rubber band,
I found a perfume bottle.
There's lots and lots still left inside
so I put it in my sock.

Yes, dear. Lovely.
Move back a bit.
What else is in this smelly sock?

Before I found the perfume bottle,
I found some chewing gum.
It was wasted in the gutter
so I put it in my sock.

Oh no!
Well, you can't eat that and live.
What else is in this sticky sock?

Before I found the gum,
I found some real false teeth.
I thought Granny would find them useful
so I put them in my sock.

Oh goodness! How kind,
but I rather hope someone
will claim them back.
What else is in this snappy sock?

Before I found the real false teeth,
I found one more thing.
A handkerchief, hardly used at all
so I put it in my sock.

Horrors!
That's terrible!
Get rid of it at once.
Are you sure there's nothing else?

Nothing else but a hole in the heel.
It isn't very big.

What a relief!
Ten treasures in your sock.
What will you do
with the things in your sock?

I shall put
the pig in my farmyard,
the button on my coat,
the marble in my pocket,
the key in my secret box,
the rubber band around my hand,
and the perfume bottle on my shelf.
I can't keep the chewing gum,
or the teeth or the handkerchief,
but you can share the frog.
I'll put it in the garden.

And do you know what I will do?
I think I'll wash your sock.